AFTER THE SOLSTICE

AMANDA CECELIA LANG

AFTER THE
SOLSTICE

M Y FAMILY SPENDS the first week of every summer in the coastal metropolis of Santa Barbara, part of the territories once known as the United States. In our world without borders, we're free to vacation anywhere we dare explore. The Great Pyramid, the Great Wall, the whole great, big, beautiful planet.

But tradition is tradition.

Come June 21 of any year, the Soleil family can be found in room 207 of the historic Motel 6 California. You can set your calendars by us. My parents come for the virtual galleries and high-fusion dining—and, of course, to celebrate their storybook love in the city where it all began. Me, I spend my overheated days alone on a crowded public beach, aching for excitement, chasing those elusive heartbeat moments, dying to see *Him* again. My mystery man. My parents say every moonstruck romantic needs one.

And indeed, our gravitational pull rivals the moon and the tides, the ebb and flow of a cosmic dance, two celestial bodies forever reaching for sweet, elusive embrace. I don't know his name or where he's from, only that fate aligns for us every summer solstice, the longest day of the year. Though, our close encounters have always felt surreal and fleeting.

Almost mythical.

.   .   .

I first met Him the year I turned fifteen.

The day was every other day I'd ever spent on that depressingly familiar beach. I kept to the popular dress code: designer bikini, SPF 50, the latest generation of holo-glasses. Buttery sunshine melted into my skin—though, naturally, I ignored sand and surf in favor of the social and news feeds sliding across my holo. The first juicy ripples of a scandal were stirring around the New World Commissioners that day. I can't say what inspired me to hit pause and peer beyond my holo.

Maybe because he looked so inevitable, so riveted.

A thrill of déjà vu trembled through me—which was ridiculous because the young man standing in the sand beside me was unlike anyone I'd ever seen.

He was wearing simple gray-blue clothing too bulky for beach wear. Olive skin with an odd ashy translucency. Pale hair shaved in patterns close to the skull. I couldn't place him. Not his heritage. Not even his age. His face appeared sharp-edged, oddly sage but youthful. Sloe eyes concealed a hardened gleam. And he held a journal. An *actual* leather and paper journal.

He stared reverently at the ocean as if witnessing it for both the first and billionth time. His fascination had me pulling off my holo. I blinked, dazzled by sunlight on water, wondering what he saw.

The ocean looked the same as always.

This stranger was the anomaly. The only person on the beach—probably in all of Santa Barbara—without a holo at the ready.

But there was something else: the light struck Him differently. While everyone around us shone in sunshine, he shone in ... I didn't *know* what. I must've gasped or choked on a hello, because he startled and turned my way.

And we stumbled into each other's eyes, lost and found, quick as that.

A heartbeat moment.

I had no other words to describe it. At fifteen, my only close encounters came in the serial romance holos I devoured. Wistful, eternal, fated. It didn't feel real. He sank to his knees and reached out as if to caress my face.

"I found you," he whispered, his accent a mystery.

"You certainly did." I giggled, young, awkward, already falling.

A breath shy of my lips, he jerked his hand away, perhaps realizing how inappropriate he was acting.

We were strangers, after all.

The steel returned to his expression, bright and jagged. Except it wasn't *steel*, not exactly. I'd seen eyes like his before. Took a second, but I placed that haunted look from the history holos. He reminded me of uniformed soldiers. The ones from bygone photographs, back before the Universal Peacetime Accord was signed into existence. Brave but heart torn, noble heroes after they kissed their true loves farewell. Would they survive? Would war murder the romance?

"Forgive me." He stood and backed away. He watched me, pained, studying me as he had the sea—as if witnessing me for the first and billionth time. Were those tears? "Look at you, how truly alive you are, how lovely ..."

Then he turned and ran.

I watched Him go, mystified and pleasantly flustered.

"He mistook me for someone else," I told the puzzled beachgoers who glanced up from their holos. I didn't think to chase Him.

Only inside did an echo stir, a near-silent voice calling to me from later years, suggesting this was the start of something transcendent.

He disappeared around the far cliffs and the day continued almost as if he had never been. A most vivid daydream.

I wondered if I would ever see Him again.

•   •   •

Naturally, I did. Exactly one year later.

Sixteen and sunbathing on the same beach, under the same sky. Designer bikini, SPF 50. My holo-glasses sat in the sand, happily forgotten. My attention felt sharper that year, sly to the world's many layers—even if I hadn't yet found a way to peel them back.

I watched the tide just as my mystery man had, waiting to see something remarkable. But for all I imagined I saw, the ocean churned as it always did. Frothy waves lapping the sand, pulling back again.

When he appeared around the far cliffs, it felt as if a year had never passed.

A thrill ignited inside me. Time turned our fairytale pages backward. He looked exactly the same, right down to his simple blue-gray clothing and leather journal. As if he'd run away a heartbeat earlier, made it to the other side of those rocks, then decided to come right back to me.

Ridiculous, of course.

I'd spent an entire year wondering about Him.

He stepped into the sunshine. Didn't bother shading his eyes as he scanned the beach. Our gazes locked—at least, I thought so. My pulse skyrocketed. I sat up straighter. Had the strangest feeling, like we should be running toward each other. But he turned away—the ocean stole his attention, or maybe the sky beyond. He fell into another watchful trance.

At sixteen, I wasn't bold. Wistful, hopeful, and naïve, yes. Not bold. Still, I'd spent an entire year wondering ...

I crossed into the shadow of the cliffs and marched right up to Him. Up close, he shone in his own light, breathtaking, unusual, unearthly. Completely out of place, even as he fit perfectly into my memory of Him.

"What do you see out there?" I tried to sound casual, though I'd spent countless sleepless nights rehearsing this moment.

He startled at my voice.

This time, when our eyes locked, I felt certain.

We were meant to be. I don't think either of us could breathe under the crushing force of our magnetism. Transcendent, mystifying, terrifyingly impossible.

We've been here before, I thought. And of course, I was right. On this beach, just last year.

"You again," he said, breaking the spell. "Forgive me, what did you ask?"

I blinked, blushing. Took a mortifying eternity to remember my question. "What do you see? Out there, I mean?"

"It's extraordinary." His earnest slanting smile clashed with something hidden. "I see the moon and the tide, locked forever together. Ancient waters bowing and ebbing in a timeless gravity dance with a celestial body. It's bigger than all of us, but standing here, right now, we witness each splash, each tiny miraculous moment."

"Heartbeat moments," I said.

He chuckled. "What?"

"Heartbeat moments." Nervous blood burned through me, but I'd waited a year to say this. "It's stupid, something I believed as a kid. You know, those moments that are huge but quick? The moments that make your heart pump faster. Moments you remember forever."

"Oh, I know." His gaze burned into me. "It's actually kind of perfect."

Perfect, yes. So stupid me, I broke eye contact.

At sixteen, everything about us felt charged with possibility, intimidating and overwhelming. And perfect, yes. But I didn't know what more to add to that particular heartbeat moment.

Instead, I bit my lip and pondered the pale daytime moon and the wave-crested horizon. A lovely view, certainly more magical than the one I saw before he arrived.

Problem was, nothing seemed as lovely as the deep brown eyes I was suddenly too anxious to meet. His nearness turned me hyperaware. We never touched, not that day, but my skin tingled, phantom electricity, daydreams terrifyingly close to coming alive. My heartbeat flew. Not sure how much time passed. Ten seconds, ten hours. I felt entranced.

When, at last, I found the courage to look at him, he was already gone.

My breath caught. Had he disappeared around the cliffs, like last year?

This time, I chased after Him.

But when I rounded the rocks, he was nowhere to be seen.

•   •   •

I've encountered Him many times over the years. Always in Santa Barbara, always on the summer solstice, always here upon our beach.

This place, this moment, somehow, they belonged to us.

Two strangers locked beside the tides, walking side by side in the sand. Most years we spoke in coded poetries, nothing of importance—yet speaking *with* importance, every word a vivid daydream coming wildly alive. Like old friends, like old lovers, though silent of names and aching to touch.

Like the ocean and its moon, we perfected our celestial dance.

Our intimate distance. The gravity of one tugging on the other, the other bowing and answering the call. But who's the moon and who's the water?

Perhaps we are both.

Over time, my questions about Him bloomed and turned Him mythical. I never spoke of Him, not even to my parents who understood deeply the intoxicating ambrosia of romance. He was my secret, my mystery, mine alone. So much wonder in wondering, in waiting to see.

One summer solstice, he knelt and brought his hand up as he had that first day, his fingertips almost a whisper against my lips. He smelled of sea breeze and ozone, of heartbeats thrumming the air. I started to ask who he was—who *we* were—but His secrets over-pained Him. Hushing them with a trembling smile, he led me beneath the cliffs, along a shadow-kissed path of hibiscus flowers. But when I rounded the final rocks, he was gone. Vanished.

Where he should've stood, I found a word scrawled in the wet sand.

Heartbeat ...

And so, our moments together passed.

•   •   •

The last time I saw Him was a year ago today.

The solstice sun dazzled near the horizon, animated and golden. He sat by the waterside and rose at the sight of me. He'd never looked so ragged.

"Afraid I'd missed you." His voice gave me a delicious shiver. The years between moments stretched ever longer, echoing with ever evolving desperation. His words trembled. "Today is too short."

"The longest day is short?" I laughed.

"Forgive me." He shook his head. "We've had so little time together."

Forgive Him? Our solstices have been a waking dream.

He hesitated. "When I close my eyes, you'll be gone."

"No. I'm always here, same beach, same solstice." I smiled despite a sudden unease.

He squared himself, took a step toward me. "You're not afraid?"

Such an odd question. I blushed at his closeness. "What do I have to fear?"

I wanted to say more. Ours had been the most extraordinary romance of my young life. But standing so near to Him, lost in his otherworldly slant of light, poetry began to fail me.

He frowned, always fighting some beautiful inner battle. "I have to go soon."

"Go? Go where?" A chilling idea overtook me.

Lately, the stories crossing the newsfeeds had evolved from idle gossip to theories of elite conspiracies. Many speculated that the New World Commissioners had been lying to us, though nobody could say exactly why. There was talk of misappropriated funds totaling in the trillions, rumors of global unrest ran rampant, and for the first time in almost half a century, the world felt the low murmurings of war.

Looking at Him, with his strange clothing and overcast manners, I worried he was deploying to some imminent battlefield.

"Home," he said. The word weighed upon his voice.

"Where's home?" I asked—but truly, I wasn't ready for the answer. I needed his mystery to stay alive.

"You'll find out one day."

"Then you'll be back? We'll see each other again?"

Silence distended between us, encompassed the entire beach, spanned the entire planet. The air fell so poignantly still, I imagined I heard the far-distant roar of the sun as it released itself from the day.

"You'll see me again," he promised. "But will you do something for me?"

"I ... of course."

"Kiss me farewell?"

Too breathless for words, I nodded slowly.

He tilted his head. "I want to remember you like this, only like this, Kara of the Sun."

My name. He knew my name? How? Who was this impossible stranger? Where had he come from? What did he want with me? Too many questions.

Before I could find my breath, he said, "When the world fell silent, the only sound was the beating of my heart."

Then he stepped close, and his lips brushed mine. We sparked. I have no other way to describe it. A shock of moonglow passion sizzled between us, dazzling me. Time stood still, sped up, the world tilted on its axis. His touch was the lightest I've ever experienced. Quicksilver like a midnight breeze, electric like the currents of a hummingbird pulse. My vision shimmered, aglow with the afterimages of bursting stars. We fell into each other and once there—I'd never glimpsed such bliss, such heartfelt sorrow, such transcendent depth, like witnessing the birth and death of the universe. It quickly overwhelmed me, and I closed my eyes. It was the most intensely delicate kiss of my life.

Too soon, our lips parted. He whispered *goodbye*.

I missed Him instantly, the spark of Him, the scent of his ozone. But I couldn't bring myself to open my eyes. I stood on that beach for a long eternity. When I found the courage to look around, he was gone.

I wasn't surprised.

The two of us came very close to crashing the moon into the sea that day. But only close. The ebb and pull would carry on—our endless dance would carry on.

He promised.

Time passed, a whole year, as it always does—though never one so painfully slow, if such sweet torture is possible. I worried the summer solstice would never arrive.

Now, finally, I stand in Santa Barbara once again, waiting for Him as I always have. But this year, something within me has evolved. I'm hungrier for Him than ever before. I'm ready to take us further, to see what we might become.

I feel it in the sky, in the tide, in the tugging.

Our year is now.

•   •   •

I linger on our beach and watch the ocean. I wait for Him.

To walk around the cliffs. To appear in the sand beside me.

I won't consider the possibility that I might never see Him again. Morning sunlight ripples the water, harsher than I remember. Change is everywhere; a new urgency haunts the overheated air.

This past year, the newsfeeds have splintered and darkened. Recently, the New World Commissioners admitted to funneling vast funds into a classified research and development program. Codename Beacon. They promise Beacon will enrich humanity's future. But pockets of organized radicals, the Dissidents, fear Beacon is a mass-scale weapons program, the first the world has seen in decades. Last week, the Dissidents issued a call to action: civilians must rise up before it's too late, and demand transparency. Equally disquieting are the recent abductions of top world officials, scientists, scholars, and sometimes their entire families. The Commissioners blame the Dissidents for these violent disappearances—though the rebellion has yet to claim responsibility or issue any new demands.

It's as if the entire world is holding its breath, waiting for what comes next.

But my father has advised me not to worry about such things. He says now is the time to focus on my own bright future. I'm a woman now, newly graduated from university. In the fall, I'll travel to Beijing where an internship awaits me. It'll be a life all my own, free from the traditions of my parents. I'm a fledgling testing her wings, and I've begun to realize this will be my last summer in Santa Barbara. I wish to see the world, every corner. I want to know every city and the vast cultures. I want to touch every mountain and desert and jungle. I want to walk to new beaches.

But I don't want to do this alone.

And here's that hunger again. That longing.

I still crave romance, *mystery*, but more than that I desire relationship. I want someone to stand beside me as my father stands with my mother. Someone real, someone constant.

But who'll risk these adventures with me? Who'll make the journey complete? I stare out as sunshine blazes the water. There's only one.

In a world of billions, there has only ever been one.

So, I wait.

I watch the tides. I watch the people lost inside their holos.

I brush fingertips against my lips, chasing the memory of his kiss.

The morning of the solstice warms into afternoon. Longing becomes a tender-raw ache. I won't let this ache turn to despair. I embrace hope.

And, *finally*, I see Him.

Over by the cliffs, sitting in the sand with his journal open, watching the ocean. It's as if he's always been there.

I stand, I go to Him. This is our time.

•   •   •

"I found you," I say.

He squints up at me, raising a hand to dim the sunshine. When he sees me, he smiles. Something's changed. He still exists in his own mysterious light, but those sloe eyes aren't the same. They're soft. Only soft. The turmoil has vanished. Last year's kiss has worked magic.

"Hello," he says in that elusive accent. "How are you?"

"Happy to see you. How are you?"

"I'm learning quite a lot ..." he says, almost absently. Then he peers closer. "Do you visit this beach often?"

I smile at the joke. "You could say that."

"Would you sit with me? Perhaps I could ask some questions?"

"That'd be nice." Heart pattering, I smooth my sundress and join him in the sand. He still smells of fresh ozone, like the air after a lightning strike. "Perfect day to get to know each other."

"Yes." He tilts his head back. "Would you say today is brighter than usual?"

"Brighter than any summer I remember. Perhaps that's a good omen?"

Always a mystery, he doesn't respond. He dips his head over his journal, scratching graphite across the page. I lean in, fascinated. Outside of the history holos, I've rarely seen anyone handwrite anything. Looping, graceful movements, words artful but archaic, illegible to my inexpert eye.

"What are you writing?" I wonder.

He glances up. "Everything you've said to me."

My mouth parts, and he quickly shuts the journal. "Forgive me, I'm being improper. I'll write this down later." He sets the journal aside and watches me, expectantly. "Let us talk."

Can't help it, I laugh. He's so unexpected. "Where should we begin?"

"Should I tell you my name? I believe that's customary."

I hesitate. The planet seems to spin faster, the moment suddenly surreal. I'm finally going to *know* Him. He's always felt too timeless to have a name.

His eyes are so soft. "They call me Farr."

"As in: you've journeyed far?"

"Precisely that. I've traveled the Earth. Farther than anyone I know. And you?"

"Oh, not me. Right now, Santa Barbara is the farthest I've made it. But I plan to spend my whole life exploring."

His smile falters, eyes flickering with emotions too fast to name. "No, I mean what do they call you?"

I bite back my own frown. He's asking my name? He whispered it last year, before he kissed me. *Didn't he?* Now, he looks genuinely curious. Is it possible, in the thrill of our closest encounter, that I misheard him? Or worse, that he's forgotten?

"I'm called Kara. Remember? Kara Soleil."

He tilts his head skyward, nodding slowly. "Soleil. *Kara of the Sun.*"

Chills. "That's me." I relax a little.

His attention lingers skyward. "Tell me, Kara, does today feel different?"

He senses it too. Never mind the rumors polluting the newsfeeds. Today feels charged with potential, with *connection*. Inside a wild heartbeat, I imagine a lifetime travelling the world with Him—my *Farr*. I can almost touch the daydream. Our journeys seem to echo back to me from across the decades.

Blushing heat warms my skin. "Feels like the day we've been waiting for."

He squints at me—surprised? "The day we've been waiting for? What do you mean? Tell me exactly."

My blush deepens. "I wondered if this day would ever come. Waited years to get to know you. Now here we are. Almost feels like a dream."

"You've waited years?" He's looking at me so strangely.

"Haven't you? After all our solstices. Last year, when you kissed me farewell, we *sparked* ..." I trail off. Something's wrong.

"When I kissed you farewell?" he asks, dubious. "This is my first time in Santa Barbara."

I tell myself I've misheard him, even as disbelief darkens his expression. A growing unreality nests in the pit of my chest—Farr actually seems to flicker, like a faulty holo.

"You've been here before. Right here."

He shakes his head. "You've mistaken me for someone else."

My blush becomes a burn. "There's no one else like you, Farr."

He stands abruptly, gathers his journal. "Forgive the confusion."

I scurry to my feet. "Don't lie. I know you know me."

"Forgive me, I truly don't."

"Why are you lying?"

"Forgive me." He hurries toward the cliffs. I watch him flee, stunned into paralysis. That chill of déjà vu again. We've done this a billion times. It could be our first day all over again. The endless, elusive dance starting again. His gravity tug-tug-tugging—it yanks me into action. I rush across the tide-washed sand, closing our distance once and for all.

"Farr!" I reach out; my hand closes on his shoulder and electricity prickles my fingertips like static shock. I feel him pull away—except, that's not entirely accurate.

My breath hitches, my feet sink into the sand, the beach tilts sideways—because suddenly anything is possible. Because Farr doesn't pull away.

My hand passes *through* him.

Through the odd blue-gray fabric, through flesh and muscle, through shoulder bones, down into his chest. Like a stone cutting water, like a bird falling from the sky, I pass *through* him.

And for the briefest moment, my fingertips graze the specter of his heart. It throbs once, twice. I jerk my hand away, gasping his name.

"You see now?" He faces me even as he steps away. "Kara of the Sun, whoever you are, I'm not who you think I am."

Tears blur my vision, the sunshine swims, my hand passed through him, *right through him*, inside him, his heart, I touched his heart, dazed, weak in the knees. It's too much.

The sky dims. I've never fainted before, but the daylight takes a shadowy turn and intuition braces me for impact. Still, I fight to keep eyes on him, this intimate stranger, this everlasting myth. Will he vanish again?

Before it all slips away, his words escape me. "When the world fell quiet, the only sound was the beating of your heart ..."

He stares at me, stunned. "You can't possibly understand what that means."

But I do. It means he felt something for me, once. I touched his heart.

Yes, with my *fingertips.*

My knees give out. The blazing heat overtakes me, and the daylight falls dark and quiet.

. . .

I wake to coppery light. The music of the tides.

A silver silhouette.

He stands to my left, beneath the cliffs, facing the solstice sun as it simmers above the edge of the sea. I watch him, this elusive creature, afraid to stir, afraid any deepening of breath might be enough to startle him, send him running.

He catches me watching.

"You fell faint," he says, straightening his posture. "How do you feel?"

"Mortified?" I press a hand to my shadow-haunted temple and sit up. "You're still here."

"For a while longer." He hesitates. "What you said about the world falling quiet—I told you that?"

"Yes."

He considers this. "Will you watch this final sunset with me?"

The earth spins faster—this *final* sunset? "It doesn't have to be our last."

He averts his gaze, silent.

"Farr, it doesn't have to be our last."

"I have to leave soon. Before tomorrow's end."

"Leave? Why?" I stagger to my feet. "To go where?"

"Home."

"You've said that before." Tendrils of dread creep along my spine. "Where is home, Farr?" He starts to shake his head, but I cut him off. "You promised to tell me." *One day.*

"They don't permit it. There are dangers."

"Who is *they*? The Dissidents?" I lower my voice though we're alone here below the cliffs. "Are you one of their soldiers?"

"We have no soldiers where I am."

"And where *are* you? Because my hand passed *through* you. Like a holo ..." I extend a slow hand, refusing to believe what I'm starting to believe. "Are you somewhere else?"

"Stop asking questions." He jerks away, and that old familiar turmoil lightning-flashes behind his eyes. "You won't like the answers."

"Why? What have the Dissidents sent you here to do?" I reach for him again, but falter. What if he vanishes? My hand trembles, drops away.

"I'm not a Dissident." He watches me as if I'm the one who might vanish. "You said I kissed you? That can't be true."

"You know it's true. We stood here by the water. Our kiss—Farr, I've never felt anything like it. You were electric. You were *real.*"

"That wasn't me."

"It was. I know it was."

"It wasn't me. At least—" He cuts himself off, holds it in for several crashing beats of the ocean. "At least, maybe not yet."

"Not *yet*? Farr, what does that *mean*?"

His jaw hardens. He breaks eye contact, surveying the long stretch of beach. We're not alone. People still linger, rosy and sun-kissed, toes in the sand, ignoring the golden water, noses in their holos.

"What it means is forbidden." Farr glances around.

"Who forbids it? Are you in danger?"

"Nothing like that, not exactly. The people I report to aren't a threat." His eyes settle on me—on my lips. "You knew me? Before we kissed, before I said what I said to you?"

I nod slowly. "Always so terribly mysterious, aren't you?" The sentiment becomes an accusation. "Yes, Farr, we knew each other, we've met on this beach, on this day, for years." With a sharp tongue, I tick off each turn of our endless dance. With each memory, my voice pitches higher, betraying my heartache. Because the more I say, the more Farr shakes his head.

"Forgive me, Kara. You're quite unprecedented."

"*I'm* unprecedented? Farr, who in the world are *you*? I deserve to understand."

"I'm not even certain I understand. But I'll try."

He steps barefoot to the shoreline. He leaves no footprints in the sand, and I realize with a backward shock that he never has. I can barely breathe, the tide-song crashing between my ears. I step barefoot beside him, sand between my toes.

Finally, he says, "I think the person you met, the person following you all those years, was the *future* me."

My mouth parts, but the questions choke painfully inside my throat. And with them, a sharp and instant disbelief. *The future Farr?*

"I told you," he says, "you won't like my answers. It's better this way."

"You're lying."

A billion fickle emotions shadow his sharp features. The final rays of this longest day cast jagged, kaleidoscopic gloom under his eyes, over his jaw.

"I'm not a liar, Kara," he says. "And I'll tell you everything I can. But first, let's watch the sunset."

•   •   •

"We're called Visitors," Farr tells me, standing beneath the nighttime sky.

Without the diffusion of sunlight, I see it clearer now: his silvery, otherworldly glow. He's the brightest object on this beach, brighter than the stars and the full moon dazzling over the ocean.

"I exist in actuality 213 years into your future." He pauses, waiting, I suppose, for me to call him a liar again.

"Go on," I say.

He nods. "Currently, my physical body floats inside a liquid pod known as the Corporeal-Transmigration Chamber—the most technologically advanced creation mankind has ever imagined. It's the product of ten generations of collective research and development."

I gasp. "Do you mean Project Beacon?"

He goes rigid. A parade of shadows flickers behind those sloe eyes.

"Partly," he admits. "My people are a distant offshoot of Beacon. But let me explain. The body you see is a corporeal-spectral projection. Similar to the holo-devices that are abundant in your time. Instead of projecting light particles, the C-T Chamber sends human consciousness backward into time, merging the mind with preexisting atoms, forming a semitangible display—"

I press a palm against my forehead. Beacon isn't a weapons program—it's a *time travel* program? Like something from the old sci-fi holos. "Semitangible?"

"Physically, as I exist in your time, I'm what the ancients might've called a ghost. That's why your hand cut through me. However, in certain circumstances, Visitors can concentrate our energy to manipulate physical matter. We can't sustain it for long; it drains our power. But it can be done." He hesitates. "Would you like a demonstration?"

"Yes."

He takes a deep breath—or seems to—then reaches for my hand. His fingertips eclipse mine, passing *right through*. Bone, tendon, flesh. Similar to the organ I felt beating inside his chest. Here but not here.

I whimper.

"Kara."

He reaches for me again. I don't know what changes, but this time, we *spark*. We connect. His fingers twine around my own and he squeezes. Every nerve in my body tingles, spitfires, flares, almost drops me to my knees.

He must see the faintness in me. He releases my hand. His light flickers.

"Do you see now?" he says. "How the kiss we shared felt real?"

It was *real!* I want to shout it. Instead, I brush shaky fingertips across my lips. Tears curse my eyes, casting haunting auroras atop my vision, tripling and doubling Farr. I blink, and he is the only one. But he'll only ever be a projection.

An illusion.

"Why?" I whisper, clutching my heart close. "Why are you here?"

Another hesitation. "Our purpose as Visitors is to observe the planet as it once was. We are historians. We have specialties. Some of us observe geological, environmental, and biological shifts, while others are more concerned with human events."

I shake my head, but he keeps talking.

"I oversee a little of everything. You might call me a scout. I've journeyed farther back than any other Visitor." He smiles ruefully, gaze turning inward. "You'd be amazed at all I've witnessed, Kara. Sometimes it does feel like a dream. Isn't that how you put it?"

I bite my lip. "I don't think we're talking about the same thing."

"Perhaps not." He frowns but continues on.

"The planet as it once was fascinated   me. Would you believe that I watched the construction of the pyramids? I was there during the completion of the Coliseum and the Great Wall. Visitors like me have witnessed the first and final years of countless great civilizations. I've seen ash fall at Pompeii and Indian Ocean tsunamis wash away entire coastal cities. I've been astounded and humbled. I saw the asteroid that killed the dinosaurs explode into the Yucatan Peninsula. It hung like a second sun in the sky for weeks before it struck ..."

He trails off. Do I believe him?

"The dinosaurs?" It's impossible to ignore the falling sensation inside my chest. A Visitor from the future? This is an elaborate joke. Maybe he's part of some modern-day R and D team testing out the latest holo tech. He's probably a few miles away, holed up in some laboratory. He's trying to impress me, or chase me away, or I can't imagine what. But dinosaurs? "That's sixty-five million years ago."

"I know it sounds incredible."

My fingertips still tingle from his touch. He seems so tangible, this enigma with ashy olive skin and pale hair carved with exotic patterns. This being who shines with silver light and doesn't leave any footprints when he treads the beaches of the past.

"Why are you telling me this, Farr, if it's forbidden?"

"Because I've journeyed farther, Kara." He watches the moonlit ocean with an inward gaze. "Four hundred fifty million years, to the late Ordovician period, to witness a gamma ray burst hit the Earth, to study it. Bursts are created when dead stars collide. The resulting explosion is the most powerful force in the known universe, second only to the Big Bang. The energy released is so titanic it can outshine an entire galaxy of stars."

I hold my breath. In a billion daydreams, this isn't how I imagined this encounter. "I don't understand what this has to do with us."

He turns to me, squares his shoulders like a soldier. "I was sent back to monitor the moment of impact, nothing more. The burst hit the planet like a laser and burned away Earth's atmosphere in a matter of seconds. It was the brightest light storm this world has ever experienced. If I had witnessed it with my physical eyes, I'd have been instantly blinded. But I saw it all. The innumerable species evolving in the oceans bobbed to every surface, dying of radiation exposure almost instantly. In the moments after the blast, I stood on that ancient shore, and I confess to you, Kara, the loneliness was profound. There wasn't another living soul to be found. The entire planet had fallen quiet."

"Except for the beating of your heart."

"Except for the beating of my heart." He smiles at me, ruefully. "When I returned to the present—my time—for debriefing, I relayed every detail of my observations. Everything but that one moment. I don't know why. I'd never withheld anything before." Vulnerability washes over him. He drops his gaze to the sand, jaw tight. "I suppose everyone deserves something that belongs only to them."

It's amazing. I can't look away from this person who, like a dream, is real but not real. The gravity between us tugs my breath.

I understand what he's saying. After all, haven't I kept him all for myself? Farr found me on every summer solstice—and yet, who have I told about our encounters? Not close friends, not even my parents, those unabashed romantics. Sometimes life hands you a gift, a wonder, an experience, made for you alone. To share it, to let someone else hold it and examine it, would be to tarnish it. I understand why Farr kept his moment to himself, and yet.

And yet.

"You shared it with me?" I whisper.

"Yes, it appears I did. Or will."

"Why?"

His smile dies. The way he's suddenly looking at me makes me want to sob and fall into his arms all at once. It's as if he finally sees me. He raises a slow hand to my face, a gesture of his I'm achingly familiar with. Only this time, he doesn't stop a breath away from my skin. We *spark* and he traces soft fingertips along the curve of my cheekbone, brushing tears from my bottom lashes. I go very still, drinking in his touch, my entire body blushing, full of lightning.

Do I believe him?

Yes, yes, I do. A part of me—some timeless, transcendent echo of who I was and who I will be—nods in silent understanding. Have I always sensed the truth, this gossamer déjà vu? I want to believe I have.

"Visitors are permitted to interview citizens of yesteryears," he says. "As long as we don't interfere. In all my travels, I've never met anyone like you, Kara. Someone so astonishing you'll inspire my future self to return to you again and again."

He traces my neck, my shoulder, and my arm. I shiver, whimpering on the inside as he clasps my hand sweetly, impossibly, in his own.

"You asked why I would share such a personal moment with you?"

I can only nod, too lost inside the fathoms of this dreamscape.

"I think it was so that when you found me today and told me of our strange encounters, I would believe you, Kara of the Sun. And devote future travels to you."

•   •   •

The starry sky blazes above us and as nighttime deepens, the beach becomes our oasis. An eastward dancing breeze cools the air by the water; ruffling my sundress, prickling my bare shoulders. Nights like this were born for warm embraces, so I try not to shiver. We leave only a single set of footprints.

We follow the slow curve of the shoreline, and after a spell, Farr says, "It's a lovely night."

"Insanely," I agree. Other men might use such words to fill the silence, but there's an earnestness to Farr. He possesses at once a childlike awe and a wise attentiveness. Watching him watch the sea is an odd, sweet pleasure. Somehow, I've already grown accustomed to his otherworldly glow and the way it reflects softly off my skin. Honestly, my senses keep lying, insisting he could lift me into his arms and spin me around. We could dance. Together, we could break the tide.

"You have a way about you," I say. "As if you see some hidden beauty."

"Visitors are trained to be observant. But it doesn't take a practiced eye to recognize beauty."

"Maybe not." I bite my smile. "But how does your eyesight work? How does any of this? Am I a projection to you, some kind of ultrafuturistic holo? When you took my hand before, could you actually feel me or—"

"Kara, stop. This is all very real for me." He tilts his head toward the moon and breathes in. "Sometimes the sensations can be overwhelming. So many new perfumes carried on a gust of wind. Such myriad colors."

"You don't have color in the future?"

"Of course we do." He drops his chin back down. Our bare feet step in rhythm across the sand. "But every era is different."

I nod. For all his talk of existing in the moment, I sense his thoughts wandering again. New shadows haunt his eyes, soldier shadows. "What you're doing right now, telling me all this—the people you report to forbid it?"

"Technically, yes, but ..."

"But?"

"They cannot observe the past. They only know what Visitors tell them."

"How long have you been a Visitor?"

"I was born into the program."

I try not to betray my shock. "They bred you for this?"

"I'm genetically equipped to handle the stresses the C-T Chamber puts on the brain. Being a Visitor is held as a great honor."

"Of course, I'm sorry. It's just you've been doing this since you were a child? I can't imagine what that would be like. To have seen so much."

"Sometimes, it's as if I've lived a thousand lifetimes except my own."

I swallow. "That sounds ..." Awful and lonely and somehow heroic.

"It's an honor to spend one's life exploring the past," he says again.

"Is the future so dull?" I half tease. He doesn't smile.

"Not dull. Only ..." He stares seaward. "There's much to admire in the past."

As we continue along the shoreline, the moon rising ever higher, he tells me how he felt the ground shake at Cape Canaveral on the day Apollo 11 reached for the moon. He was there, off the coast of Sri Lanka, when the Wanderer 3 exploded, ending the last of the Mars programs. He's watched great people lay the cornerstones of great monuments and once stood in Venture Square amid a crowd of millions as the Universal Peacetime Accord was signed into existence and the first New World Commissioners were sworn in.

"But it's the little moments," Farr says. "So many things that define humankind have beginnings most people rarely consider. Do you know, we believe I was there for humanity's first kiss? It wasn't between a man and woman, like you might imagine. But a mother and her infant child. A simple gesture of love." He stops walking and faces me. "It's the small moments that matter, Kara. Unexpected bursts of inexplicable beauty. Do you believe that?"

I nod. I could fall into those sloe eyes. "The heartbeat moments."

"The heartbeat moments."

Water splashes my ankles, warm, foamy, full of moon glow. Sand swirls around my feet only to disappear as the sea pulls back again, the faithful ebb and flow.

"Tell me about the happiest moments of your life," Farr says.

"Happiest moments?" I give a little laugh. Does right now count? A lightning storm of summer solstices flashes to mind. Sure, my past encounters with Farr drove me wild with joy—but I've already told him all that. Besides, the history of this beach extends well beyond when I was fifteen and a mysterious stranger stepped into my life. I grin.

"My parents met on this beach, too. Well, actually ..." I point to distant lights coasting lazily out on the water. "On a tour boat called the SS *Lovecraft*, if you can believe it. They were attending university on separate sides of the continent, but my father didn't let that stop him. Said she was the only girl out of billions to make him go starry-eyed. He transferred schools, and after graduation, they returned to Santa Barbara for their honeymoon."

"And they've returned every year since?" Farr guesses.

"Every year. This time, they're taking another cruise, spending their anniversary on the water. But my earliest memory is watching them play chase on this beach." I close my eyes, summoning the warmth of long-ago sunshine. "Whenever he caught her, he'd swing her around. Then he'd kiss the tip of her nose and they'd run and crash into the ocean. Their laughter filled the entire world. Never seen two people so in love, not even in the old romance holos ..." I trail off, opening my eyes, returning to our moment.

"You admire their relationship."

"More than anything." I cough out a reflective chuckle, surprised by what I'm about to confess. "I know they love me, of course they do. But first and foremost, my parents are devoted to each other. I daydream about finding love like that. The world's more vibrant when you're not alone, you know? And I plan to see every corner of it."

I don't realize how immeasurably I've fallen into the warm glow of Farr's gaze until he turns away. He starts to say my name, then hardens his jaw. I know what he's wondering, two hundred years in the future—because I'm wondering myself.

But this is our heartbeat moment, our solstice, our longest day.

"My father says people have forgotten the power of courtship," I say. "He told me medieval knights would sometimes pursue the same lady for an entire lifetime without getting close enough to kiss her hand. Some wrote long letters on the battlefield, more poets than soldiers. Their women tucked those letters in their corsets to keep their knights close." I press a fist against my chest. "Don't know if that's true, but I want it to be."

"Your father got it right."

"About the letters?"

"About it all, Kara of the Sun."

And all at once, the two of us are burning, locked in a standoff. I curl my toes into the wet sand. My fingertips prickle, anticipating the spark of his touch. My bloodstream electrifies, the night tilts sideways, the urge to tangle this man in my arms is dizzying. Our next breath fills with unspoken poetry, and our gravity turns solar.

We collide.

Not merely a spark.

If passion could be translated into a celestial event, we would light up the galaxy.

Farr grasps the back of my neck and I cling to his shoulders, and for the sweetest, most terrible instant, we pass through. Ghostly fingertips graze my spine, and my own hands slip along the fibrous muscles tensing inside his upper arms. The air around us crackles, then in a flash my skin radiates beneath the featherlight pressure of his touch.

This time, I don't dare close my eyes.

His mouth lights me up, gentle and ravenous and completely electric. Exactly like our first time—of course, for this version of Farr, this *is* our first kiss. It's enough to inspire a transcendent thrill of déjà vu. Spinning, falling. Kisses like this were made to exist forever, outside the trappings of space and time. I peer into him and imagine I glimpse all his wonders. That ancient day when the planet fell silent. In this too brief eternity, awash in the sensation of him, I memorize the sound of his heartbeat.

He's witnessed a thousand lifetimes, but this kiss is his own. *Our* own.

I'm stunned when he abruptly pulls away, fighting gravity, letting me go.

"Unfathomable," he whispers—but with each syllable, static crackles his voice and his glow flickers. For several insidious seconds, he simply vanishes.

"Farr!"

"Still here," he says, shivering back to solidity, dimmer than before, glimmering sporadically, but still here. "Can't do that too often, forgive me."

I'm afraid to ask, but ..." How long can you stay here, before your power expires?"

"Travels are generally calibrated to last a little over a day. Manifesting can drain minutes, sometimes hours depending on intensity."

"But you can always come back?"

He nods—but always with him, I sense a hesitation.

"Here, sit." I gesture toward an abandoned beach chair. He chuckles when he realizes my concern.

"In this form, I don't need rest." But he takes a seat in the sand, inviting me to join him. "Tell me more, Kara of the Sun. Tell me your happiest days."

And so, I do. I fill the remaining hours of the night with the wistful adventures of a girl who's always felt achingly out of place—dare I think it?—out of *time*. A girl whose farthest travels have been journeys through old holo books and movies and sims. My stories don't include celestial events or rocket ships, but Farr listens avidly, as if he absorbs not just my words, but my nuances.

Our understanding of each other deepens, and so do the hours. Out on the sea, the Earth's subtle curve meets the sky. We settle onto our backs and watch the slow spin of the stars. Our breath matches rhythm with the water. My eyelids grow heavy. Fighting my own dimming, I whisper, "You'll still be here when the sun comes up?"

"I won't leave your side, Kara."

Drifting, wrapped in a cool breeze and the fiercest heartbeat sensation of Farr's closeness, it's tempting to pretend, to imagine, to believe there's a tangible future for us.

So, I do.

For what remains of this night, I exist inside the daydream.

·　　　·　　　·

I jerk awake, dazed, spinning. It takes several frantic heartbeats to place myself on this beach. Sitting up, shaking the sand from my hair, the thrumming tension doesn't dissipate. Something is wrong, something is wrong, something is—

Then I remember. A backwash of memories crashes over me. I scan the beach—people everywhere, huddled in small groups—my heart pounds in my throat. At last, I spot Farr's silhouette down by the shoreline. He stands with his journal open, head tilted skyward. He still leaves no footprints.

Standing, smoothing my sundress, I go to wish him a good morning. The words fade to a gasp.

The sky.

How could I have missed it, even for a second?

The sky.

It dazzles. I shield my eyes with one hand. My knees weaken, teetering between awe and the certainty that this is the last of a series of extraordinary dreams.

Horizon to horizon, ribbons of living color streak the sky.

Wavering, incandescent, *electric* color: greens, indigos, turquoises. The strange ethereal light casts the surrounding cliffs and palms and people in a floating neon haze, an unfathomable beauty.

"Farr?" I startle him. He tucks his journal away.

"Kara ..."

"What am I seeing?" My awe trembles; I can't help it. "It's so beautiful."

"Forgive me," he whispers, ghostly—not translucent, but a vision of my past. That haunted stranger who seemed so exquisitely tortured every summer solstice. He's standing here now. Refusing to meet my gaze.

"What is it? What is it, Farr? *What is it?*"

"An aurora borealis."

I blink. He's right. Northern lights—on southern beaches? In the daytime? Icy dread cycles through me, turning like gears in a clock, backward, backward through every epoch Farr has witnessed. Pyramids, rocket launches, peace treaties—tsunamis, earthquakes, asteroids. Monumental dates in Earth's history.

The Visitors observe moments of epic creation.

And profound destruction.

I've been asking the wrong questions.

The waves crash in.

This isn't simply an aurora borealis.

The waves crash out.

"Why are you here, Farr?" I whisper, but the silence paining his expression tells me I won't like his answer. "What are you supposed to witness?"

Kaleidoscopic blues and greens twist and shiver across his face. My fingertips spark as he takes my hand. Disbelief blurs my vision. Why is Farr crying?

"Forgive me, Kara. I didn't know how to tell you. I wanted your final day to be bliss, everything you've wished for."

"You didn't just say this is my final day. You didn't!" I try to pull away, even as his hand tightens, sparks pulling through me, a crackling magnetic current.

"You deserved a beautiful night," he insists, flickering, not letting go.

"I deserve to know what this is!"

He regards me with secret intensity even as I taste the ghosts of first kisses upon my lips.

"A gamma ray burst," he relents, eerily technical. "The aurora borealis is Earth's atmosphere reacting with the first wave of radiation."

My spine ices over. A gamma ray burst? Like the one that made the planet fall silent? Farr said it burned away the atmosphere, poisoned the air and seas with a flash-bomb of radiation. This can't be. The universe shone so friendly last night. Farr was supposed to be here to fall in love.

There are too many people on the beach this morning: lovers and friends, families with young children, laughing, talking excitedly, their holos forgotten for once as they admire the mysteriously lovely sky.

But they don't know about the sound of silence.

"How long?"

"Kara ..."

"How long do we have, Farr?"

"Less than an hour."

It's not every day the man I've fallen in love with tells me it's all been a lie.

An hour? I slump to my knees. Farr tries to hold me up, but I slice through him, bones and tendons, and he flickers. He reaches for me again, but I pull away. Sand needles my knees as I stare at the sea, finally seeing it.

The fragility of it all.

"You have to go back," I say weakly. "Go back in time and warn them. The New World Commissioners, they could—"

"They already know, Kara." Farr drops down beside me. "They've known for decades this was coming, that there's no way to stop it. The stars that caused this burst were much closer than the one that caused the Ordovician mass extinction—the damage will be exponentially worse. All life forms existing less than seven miles below the surface will go extinct." His voice buzzes inside my head, distant and tinny. Coupled with the otherworldly diffusion of greenish-blue light, unreality takes on a whole new dimension. "Forgive me, Kara. Today's the day the world ends."

"But you exist," I lift my chin. "There are people in the future."

"Only a handful of us, and only in a single location. Project Beacon is a massive underground ark beneath the Himalayas, a city where what remains of humanity lives in waiting. Our surface is scorched and barren and our skies rage with electrical storms. We experience a blue-and-green Earth only through our travels into the past."

My vision swims, my bloodstream numbs, all the symptoms of despair. All the politicians, the scientists and scholars, all those kidnappings that have become banner stories on the newsfeeds—they weren't kidnappings at all. The highest echelon of people tasked to serve mankind have gone underground. They've abandoned us.

"It'll be fast," Farr promises. "I won't leave you."

But he already has.

The future Farr, the stranger who'll visit me in my younger incarnations, knows the date of my death and will never try to warn me. Never once warn the billions and billions who'll lose their lives today.

Nearby, an unsuspecting couple passes into the frame of our moment. Kicking up sand, laughing blithely, darting around each other in a game of chase. At once, the man lunges forward and twirls her into his arms. They marvel at the sky and kiss each other bathed in a shimmering blue-green glow. I look away.

"My parents, I should warn them ..." I fumble in my shoulder bag for my holo-glasses, then murmur a voice command. Nothing happens. The battery's dead. The *charge battery* prompt has gone black too.

"Electronics won't work," Farr says, every word cruel with apology. "An electromagnetic pulse shorted everything out."

I set the glasses on the sand and slowly rise to my feet.

Farr steps in front of me, and his desperate chivalry presses heavy upon my chest. How many love stories end in tragedy? Tragedy sweetens romance, isn't that what they say? Standing face to face with Farr—this inexplicable stranger who hid the end of the world to give me the loveliest night of my life—I find it impossible to breathe. Impossible to speak. Heartache fills my throat. Fills our moment.

"We'll never see the world together."

"Kara ..."

I sprint from the shore. I don't look back—I barely look forward as I stagger past all the people who'll soon be corpses. Farr calls my name, chasing me but never truly touching the sand. I run faster, time running out. I've been coming to this beach my entire life, but suddenly I can't recall which path leads to our historic motel on the edge of Santa Barbara's silver metropolis. My feet race on autopilot. The glass-and-steel cityscape shines blue-green and hazy. Surreal shadows lace the ground. The distorted shapes of people pass me by, wavering and multilayered and doomed.

Slantwise transports and hovercraft litter the streets, powerless hunks of metal. Frustrated owners stand by with dead holos, heads craned skyward. The first murmurings of panic simmer the air, cracking veneers. Awe swiftly replaced by confusion, confusion by fear. Where are their newsfeeds and their loved ones? Holo ads no longer spring from the sidewalks, posh storefronts stand dark. The graffiti proclamations of local Dissidents paint the walls, still wet and dripping.

They tried to warn us. *Something is coming!*

Somewhere glass breaks. Somewhere men argue. Everything slips past me, people wandering lost, voices rising, my name echoing. Where am I going? Where's my aching heart leading me?

I barely remember until my hand closes around the sun-warmed doorknob of my motel room. The lock doesn't respond to my voice command. Not without power. I pound the door but don't bother shouting for my parents. They're not here. It all washes back—they're somewhere out on the ocean, waking up from their overnight cruise, finding the sky enchanted with color. At least I know they're happy. Of course they are. They're together.

Face hot with tears, I press my forehead against the door. If I was born in a luckier time, I might've forever associated the salty sea air with my first love. I taste his name on my lips, but it's not enough.

I have to find him one   last time. I turn.

And he's already here.

A spark. One final burst of inexplicable beauty. His hand settles on my shoulder and what we have feels so real. "I won't leave you, Kara."

•　　　•　　　•

We stand atop the cliffs overlooking our beach and our ocean and our sky.

I don't know how much time I have. Not long.

"I can go back in time and warn you," Farr says, searching, hoping, still trying to fix this. "If you could somehow get your family into Project Beacon—the life of the first survivors is a brutal one, but at least it's a life. I could go back ..."

Perhaps he could. But would I even believe him? Without seeing the sky burn with cosmic color, would my fifteen-year-old self believe the world will end before she ever gets to become a part of it?

Do I even *want* her to know the end is near?

Do I want her to spend her final years knowing that billions of people are destined to die? Perhaps she could seek out members of the Dissidents, tell them what she knows. Fight to spread the word so the entire world, more than just the chosen elite, can prepare—or fall into a civil war unlike anything humanity has ever experienced.

Would there even be any humanity left in the end? What kind of life would that be for the daydreaming daughter of a baker and a philosophy professor? Would she even stand a chance? Is that what I want my final years in this still beautiful world to be? A futile fight for a chance to live in an underground coffin, scrabbling for survival with the broken remnants of humanity?

Or do I spare her? After all, ignorance has been bliss.

I reach for him, my mystery man. My fingertips pass through his shoulder, grazing his heart. It throbs one, twice ...

"Don't change anything," I say.

I sense his devastation even as his fingertips spark against the fragile curve of my throat. "You are an unfathomable beauty, Kara of the Sun."

He kisses me.

He doesn't watch the end of the world.

He gazes into me, like he gazes into the ocean. As if he's witnessing me for the first and billionth time. As if I'm the beginning he's spent his life searching for.

"You'll find me again," I whisper. My final words. A comfort for Farr, this soul so suddenly lost in time. And a comfort for myself.

Hands that cannot touch can still reach.

With this as my wish, I extend my undying dreams backward into the past. I offer myself this gift. This gift of gossamer mystery and ageless romance.

This gift of Farr.

A heartbeat moment later, a flash as brilliant as the Bang that started us all takes first my sight and then my future.

But we still have our solstices. And one perfect night. I hold on to that.

And as I collapse through the peaceful illusion of Farr's arms, I know he'll stay with me long after my heart and our planet fall silent.

ABOUT THE AUTHOR

Amanda Cecelia Lang is a horror author and aspiring time-traveler from Colorado. Her stories haunt the dark corners of many popular podcasts, magazines, and anthologies, including *The Deadlands, Gamut, Ghoulish Tales, Cast of Wonders, Uncharted, Dark Matter*, and *Flame Tree's This Way Lies Madness*. Her short story collections, *Saturday Fright at the Movies: 13 Tales from the Multiplex* (Dark Matter INK) and *The Library of Broken Girls: Stories of Survival* (Gateway Literary), are available everywhere nightmares are sold. You can stalk her work at *amandacecelialang.com*—just don't be surprised if she leaps out at you from the shadows.

YOU MIGHT ALSO ENJOY

DALLIANCES
Spring 2025

Dalliances celebrates all kinds of love and relationships, from love bringing a ghost back to life, to finding love in an elevator, to true love between women—a variety of short stories about romance and deep friendships.